STARTING LETTERING

Fiona Watt and Patricia Lovett

Designed by Vicki Groombridge

Illustrated by Sue Stitt

Photographs by Howard Allman

Series editor: Cheryl Evans

Contents

Starting out

In this book you will find lots of different ways of lettering. On these pages you will find some of the things you can use to do your lettering. There are also some important tips to help you.

Bright pencils

Gold or silver pens

Thick felt-tip pens

Thin felt-tip pens

Paintbrush

Things you can use

You can do lettering on all kinds of paper. If you use bright paper, test your pen or pencil on it first so that you can see if it will show. You can buy different pencils, pens and crayons from art stores and stationary departments.

For some of the projects you will also need things like a pair of scissors, a ruler and an eraser.

If you don't have the same type of pen that is used for a project in this book, just use another one.

Left-handers

If you are left-handed, lay the side of your hand on the paper as you write.

Hold your pencil so that your hand is below, and a little to the left, of your writing.

Hold your pencil with your fingers 2-3cm (¾ -1¼ in) away from the point, like they are in the picture.

Lay your paper so that the left-hand corner is higher than the right-hand corner.

Plain gift wrap

Textured paper with a bumpy surface.

White paper from an art pad

Patterned gift wrap

Bright art paper

It is difficult to write on shiny paper. Use it for letters which you cut out or glue letters onto it.

Before you begin

Read through the list at the beginning of each project and make sure that you have everything you need.

Try to work in a bright place so that your hand doesn't make shadows on your letters.

Always remember to put the lid back on a pen when you have used it. Wash any brushes you use.

Right-handers

Hold your pencil between your thumb and first two fingers, about 1½cm (½in) from the point.

Your hand should be below, and a little to the right, of your writing. Lay the paper as it is in the picture.

Rest the pencil in the V-shape between your thumb and your first finger.

Highs and lows

Letters are made up of different lines and shapes. Some letters are small and round and others are tall. When you begin lettering try to keep your letters even. You can do this by writing between lines.

On these pages you will need:
A pencil, a ruler and an eraser
Different shades of paper
Bright felt-tip pens or pencils
A large plate

Capital letters fill the top two lines only.

You can change the shape of capital letters by making them thin or wide.

You could add a dot at the end of every line of your letters.

Starting out

Write small letters between these lines.

Make these parts touch the middle lines.

With a pencil and ruler draw four lines the same distance apart. Write some small letters.

Make all tall letters apart from 't' touch the line at the top. Make 't' a little shorter.

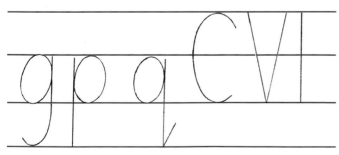

When you draw letters like these (see below), don't make the letters too close together when you begin.

Letters like g, p and y have a 'tail' which hangs down. Make the tails touch the bottom line.

Start a word with a capital letter or use all capitals, but don't put a capital in the middle of a word.

Around and around

1

2

Draw a letter with one pen. Choose another one and draw around the outside of the letter.

Choose a third pen and go around the second outline. Keep on going using different pens.

Wavy letters

1

Draw faintly with a pencil.

Draw a wavy line across your paper. Make it wiggle like a snake but don't make the curves too steep.

2

Make the lines follow the same wavy shape.

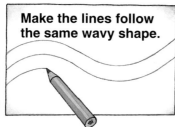

Draw another wavy line about 1cm (½in) below the first one. Add another line above and below.

3

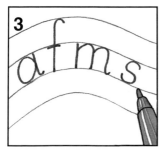

Write a wavy message between the lines. Make capital letters and tall letters fill the top two spaces.

Around the bend

1

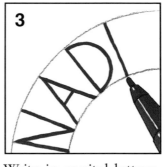

Put a large plate on your paper so that it overlaps one corner. Draw around it faintly with a pencil.

2

Pull the plate out a little and draw around it again. The space between the lines gets narrower at the ends.

3

Make your letters touch both lines.

Write in capital letters. Turn your paper as you write so that your letters stand upright between the lines.

Erase your pencil lines when the ink is dry.

5

Feathers and teeth

You can join some letter shapes together to make patterns. These patterns can also be used to draw snakes and insects or decorate other animals.

You will need:
Lined paper
White or bright paper
Felt-tip pens
A pencil

Joining up

The dotted lines show the shapes you make.

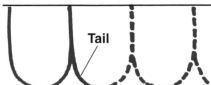

Tail

Use lined paper.

Start with a 'u' shape. Give it a curved tail. Take the tail up to the top line and write another letter 'u'.

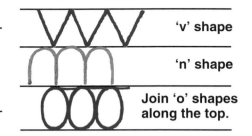

'v' shape

'n' shape

Join 'o' shapes along the top.

Try some other letter shapes. As you write, try not to take your pencil off the paper.

Creepy crawlies

For a caterpillar, draw a row of joined 'o's. Use 'L' for their feet.

To draw an insect, join three 'o's. Make the last letter big.

Add wings, feelers and legs.

Draw two rows of 'v's to make a zigzag snake.

Add a head, a tongue and eyes to your snake.

Add six legs and feelers for an ant.

For a wiggly snake, draw a row of 'n's, then a row of 'u's between the 'n's.

Feathery bird

1

With a felt-tip pen, draw the outline of a very fat bird on your paper. Add eyes, a beak and feet.

2

Use a pencil.

Add lines across its tummy. Make them about two fingers' width apart. Don't worry if they are wobbly.

3

Starting on the left, draw a row of joined letter 'u's between the lines. Try to make them all the same.

4

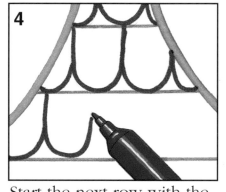

Start the next row with the top of each letter touching the bottom of the one above, as shown.

5

Keep on adding rows until you have filled the tummy. Then erase your pencil lines.

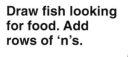

Use bright pens to fill in between the joined letter shapes.

Draw fish looking for food. Add rows of 'n's.

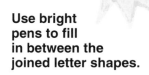

Draw or paint a crocodile with an open mouth.

Add a row of joined 'V's for spiky teeth.

7

Shapes and patterns

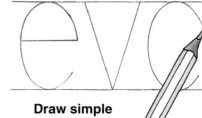

Here are some easy ways that you can make simple letters look more interesting. Before you try any of these letters, always draw faint letters in pencil as a guide (see right).

You will need:
A pencil
Pieces of paper
Felt-tip pens
An eraser
A ruler

Letter guides

1

The lines will help you to keep your letters about the same size.

Use a pencil and a ruler to draw lines which are the same distance apart all the way along.

2

Draw simple letters in pencil.

Write your letters faintly. Make them touch both of the lines and leave small spaces between them.

Use one pen to draw the outline and fill it in with another one.

Fat letters

1

Make any middle part very small.

Round end

Draw an outline around the first letter. Make the ends of the letter very round. This helps to make it look fat.

2

Erase this line.

To make the next letter lie under the first one, overlap their outlines. Erase any lines inside the first letter.

3

Add the other letters in the same way. Go over the outlines with a felt-tip pen. Erase all the pencil lines.

Block letters

1

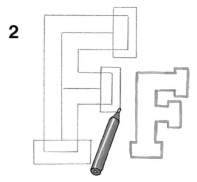

Use capital letters and give them square corners.

Write your letter guides at least a finger-width apart. Draw wide, chunky outlines around the guides.

2

Add a block shape at the ends of the letter shape. Go over the outlines with a pen. Erase the pencil lines.

No outline

Use a pen with a wide tip.

Draw a letter outline in pencil. Add diagonal stripes across it with a pen, then erase all the pencil lines.

Wiggly shapes added with a 'magic' pen (see below).

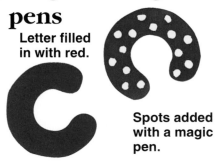

Getting bigger

1

Use a ruler and pencil.

Draw a line across your paper close to the bottom. Add another line like this, joining them at one end.

2

Keep your letters upright.

Write your letters between these lines. Make each one touch both lines. Your letters will get bigger and bigger.

'Magic' change pens

Letter filled in with red.

Spots added with a magic pen.

Try using pens which change from red to yellow, for example, when you go over them with a 'magic' pen.

9

Seeing double

Try lettering with two pencils or pens which are joined together.

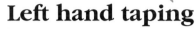

You will need:
Adhesive tape
Scissors
Two sharp pencils
Felt-tip pens
Paper

Right hand taping

If you write with your right hand, tape the pencils together like this.

The points should be like this.

If you are right-handed, hold the pencils with the points level. Tape them together in two places.

Hold the pencils in your right hand as you would normally hold just one pencil on its own.

Left hand taping

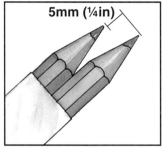

5mm (¼in)

Hold the points like this.

If you are left-handed, tape the pencils with the point of the top one 5mm (¼in) below the bottom one.

Hold the pencils as you would normally hold just one. Look carefully to see how to have the points.

Double letters

1

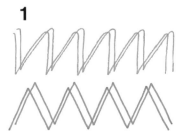

Try to keep the pencil points at the same angle.

It may feel a little odd when you write with two pencils. Begin by making patterns and shapes.

2

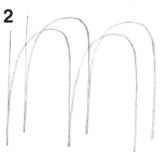

Make the letter big.

Write a letter. Don't turn your wrist as you do it. Can you see thick and thin spaces between the lines?

3

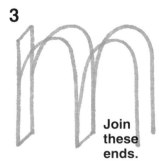

Join these ends.

Use a felt-tip pen to draw over all the lines you have made. Join up the ends of the letters.

4

Fill in the spaces between the lines. Your letters will have some lines which are thicker than others.

You can make 'see-through' letters if you don't fill in between the double lines. Don't forget to join the ends of the lines.

Fill in part of a pattern and try small letters.

Make a pen

You can make a thick double-tip felt pen from cardboard.

You will need:
Thick cardboard
15x2cm (6x¾in)
A strip of felt
10x2cm (4x¾in)
Scissors
A rubber band
Ink or food dye
An old saucer

Try some of the letter patterns on page 6.

1

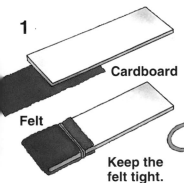

Cardboard

Felt

Keep the felt tight.

Lay the cardboard halfway along the felt, then fold the felt over. Fasten it with a rubber band.

2

Snip a V shape through the felt and the cardboard at the end. Try to make it in the middle.

3

Hold it like your double pencils.

Put a little ink or runny food dye on a saucer. Dip the tip of your 'pen' into it and write big letters.

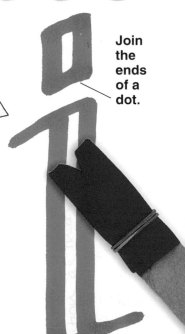

Join the ends of a dot.

11

Straight-line letters

Although some letters, such as s, b and p have curvy parts, you can make every letter using straight lines only.

On these pages you will need:
Masking tape
An unwaxed paper plate
Ready-mixed paints
Inks or food dye
Two old saucers
A small piece of sponge
Newspaper
A white candle
Paper, pencil and eraser

You'll be left with white spaces where the tape had been.

Masking tape letters

1

Use a pencil to draw the letter.

Draw a large letter on paper. Cut some tape to fit over the line where you started your letter. Press it down.

2

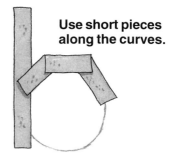

Use short pieces along the curves.

Add another piece of tape. Overlap the first one a little. Add more tape until you finish your letter.

Letter on a plate

1

Draw a big letter in the middle of the plate. Cut strips of masking tape to cover the lines.

2

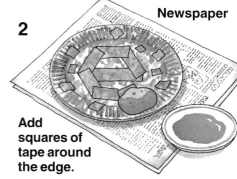

Newspaper

Add squares of tape around the edge.

Decorate the plate with more tape. Pour some paint onto a saucer. Dip the sponge into it then dab all over.

3

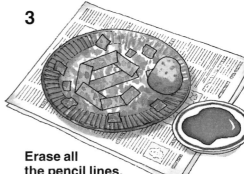

Erase all the pencil lines.

When the paint is dry, sponge on a different one in patches. When all the paint has dried, peel off the tape.

Candle letters

1

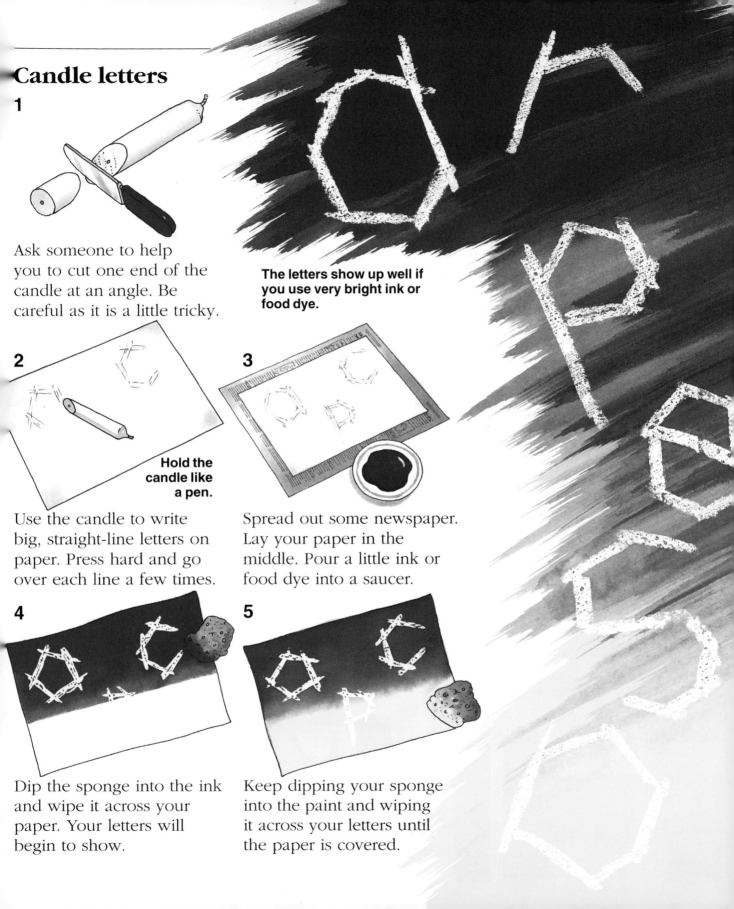

Ask someone to help you to cut one end of the candle at an angle. Be careful as it is a little tricky.

The letters show up well if you use very bright ink or food dye.

2

Hold the candle like a pen.

Use the candle to write big, straight-line letters on paper. Press hard and go over each line a few times.

3

Spread out some newspaper. Lay your paper in the middle. Pour a little ink or food dye into a saucer.

4

Dip the sponge into the ink and wipe it across your paper. Your letters will begin to show.

5

Keep dipping your sponge into the paint and wiping it across your letters until the paper is covered.

Cut it out

Another way to make letters is to cut them out, instead of writing them. You can use these letters in all kinds of ways, such as for making cards or gluing them onto project folders.

You will need:
Different types of bright paper, gift wrap or cardboard with a bumpy surface
Scissors
A pencil

1

You need to make your letters big and bold.

Draw a faint letter in pencil. Make your letter fatter by adding a straight or curvy outline around it.

Try all kinds of different shapes and styles for your letters.

2

Add any middle parts to your letter.

It's a good idea to cut around your letter roughly and then cut it out neatly.

3

Snip it inside the middle part.

If your letter has a middle part, bend the paper and make a snip. Push the scissor blade in and cut it out.

Letters on a T-shirt

You could use cut-out letters to decorate a T-shirt.

You will need:
Tracing paper
A dark felt-tip pen
Clear self-adhesive plastic
A pale T-shirt
A large piece of cardboard
Fabric paint
A thick paintbrush
Scissors and a pencil
Adhesive tape

1

Draw some very big letters on the tracing paper then draw around their outlines with a felt-tip pen.

You could cut out some shapes as well as letters.

2

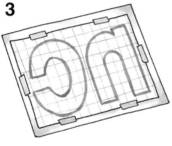

Turn the paper over so that your letters are back to front. They will be the correct way on your T-shirt.

3

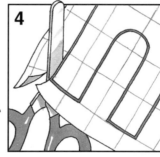

Lay a piece of self-adhesive plastic on top of your letters, with the shiny side down. Tape it on.

4

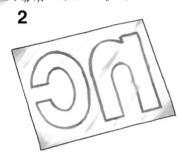

Use a pencil to trace your letters. Cut around them roughly, then cut them out very neatly.

5

Push the cardboard inside your T-shirt. Peel the backing paper off your letters and press them on.

6

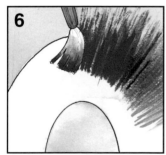

Dip your brush in fabric paint. Put the tip of it near to the edge of a letter and flick the brush out.

7

Keep on flicking the paint around the letters. Peel off all the letters when the paint is dry.

Follow the maker's instructions to 'fix' the paint.

Grow your name

It will only take a few days to grow the letters of your name using cress or mustard seeds.

You will need:
Scrap paper and a pencil
Kitchen sponge cleaning cloth
Scissors
A fine-pointed felt-tip pen
A large dinner plate
Cress or mustard seeds
A clean food tray larger than the sponge cleaning cloth
A metal spatula

1

Put the sponge cleaning cloth onto the scrap paper and use a pencil to draw around it.

2

Draw the letters of your name onto the paper. If your name has many letters, you could just draw your initials.

3

Cut out the letters. Place them on the sponge cloth and draw around them with the felt-tip pen.

4

Cut around the letters. Get someone to help you to cut out the middle pieces if there are any.

The little brown seeds are cress and the round white ones are mustard.

5

Put the letters on the plate and sprinkle them with cress seeds. Don't cover them completely.

6

Slip a spatula under each letter and lift them onto the tray. Remove any loose seeds with a wet finger.

7 **Pour the water onto the tray, not over the seeds.**

Put the tray in a warm dark place. Look at it every day and add a little water if the sponge feels dry.

8

After a few days, the seeds start to sprout. Leave the tray on a window sill until the cress grows taller.

You'll see little white roots when the seeds start to sprout.

This letter was covered in mustard seeds.

This is what cress looks like when it grows.

17

That's torn it

It can be difficult to tear neat letters from paper, but if you brush the paper with water first you'll find it's easy.

You will need:
Thin paper
Bright or patterned paper
A thin paintbrush with a pointed tip
Glue stick

1

Brush the outline on thin paper.

Dip your paintbrush into water and draw the outline of a letter. Don't make the letter too small.

2

Add any middle parts.

Brush over the outline again then let the water soak into the paper for one or two seconds.

3

Gently push the end of the paintbrush into the paper where you wrote your letter, so that the paper tears.

4

With your fingernail, gently tear around the letter shape. Keep the middle parts you tear out of any letters.

5

Glue on any middle parts in place.

Leave the paper to dry, then glue the back of it. Press it onto another piece of bright paper.

Ripped letter

You can also make bright letters using little pieces of torn paper.

1

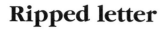

Write a large letter on the thick paper with the glue stick. Go over it again to fill in any gaps in the glue.

If you use shiny paper, draw a back-to-front letter on the back.

2

Press a paper square onto the glue at the top of the letter. Press another one on, overlapping their edges.

You could use bright paper from old magazines.

3

Keep on adding squares until the glue is covered. Do it quickly before the glue dries.

The big M was torn out and then another M was torn out carefully inside it.

These letters were glued onto bumpy cardboard. You can buy it in craft stores.

Curly whirly letters

If you bend pieces of string you'll find that you can make really curly letter shapes. You can then use them to do rubbings on paper.

On these pages you will need:
Pieces of thick string
Household glue (PVA)
Scissors
Paintbrush and paints
Paper
Thin cardboard
Wax crayons

If you use bright paper, test your crayon first to make sure that it will show.

1
Make the ends of the letter really curly.

Dip a paintbrush in the glue and draw a large curly letter on a piece of paper. Wash your brush.

2
Use more than one piece of string if you need to.

Before the glue dries, press pieces of string into it. Follow the curved lines you have drawn with the glue.

3

Leave the glue to dry. If you want to paint your letter, mix a little glue with the paint before you use it.

Tip

If your glue is in a bottle with a pointed end, use this to draw your letter instead of using a paintbrush.

Squeeze the bottle to let the glue flow.

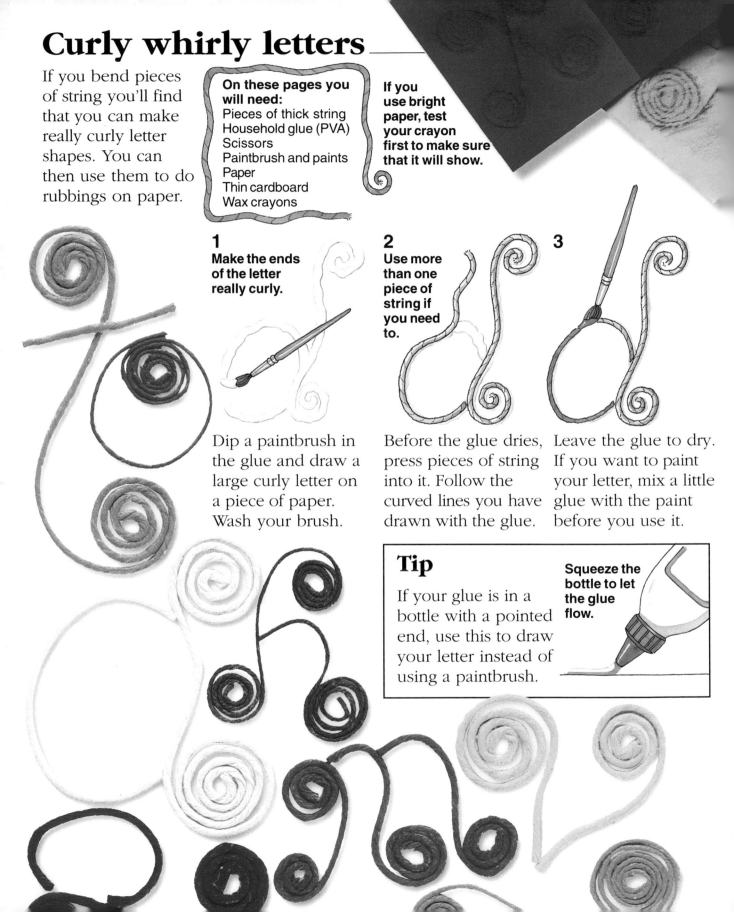

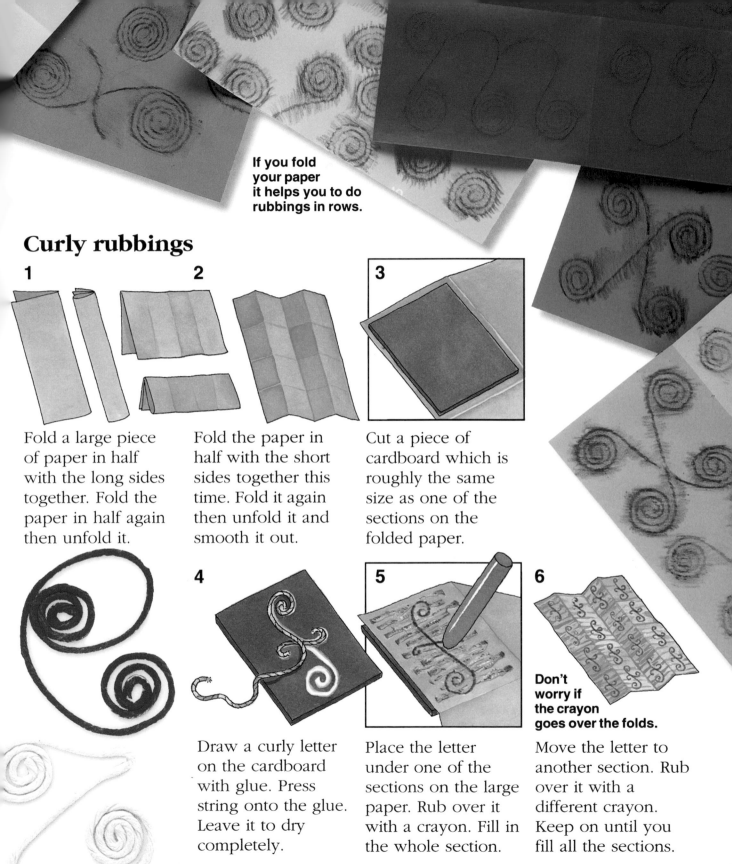

If you fold your paper it helps you to do rubbings in rows.

Curly rubbings

1

Fold a large piece of paper in half with the long sides together. Fold the paper in half again then unfold it.

2

Fold the paper in half with the short sides together this time. Fold it again then unfold it and smooth it out.

3

Cut a piece of cardboard which is roughly the same size as one of the sections on the folded paper.

4

Draw a curly letter on the cardboard with glue. Press string onto the glue. Leave it to dry completely.

5

Place the letter under one of the sections on the large paper. Rub over it with a crayon. Fill in the whole section.

6

Don't worry if the crayon goes over the folds.

Move the letter to another section. Rub over it with a different crayon. Keep on until you fill all the sections.

21

Eat your name

These letters are not only easy to make, you can eat them when you've finished.

Set the oven to 190°C, 375°F, gas mark 5 before you begin.
For about eight letters, you will need:
125g (½ cup) plain flour
50g (¼ cup) margarine
50g (¼ cup) brown sugar
A small egg, beaten
1 teaspoon of ground ginger
A greased baking tray

1

Put the margarine and the sugar together in a big bowl. Mix them until they make a creamy mixture.

2

Sift the flour.

Stir the mixture and add the egg a little at a time. Sift in the flour and the ginger into the bowl.

3

Add a little more flour if the dough feels very sticky.

Stir everything together to make a smooth mixture. Squeeze it with your hands to make a firm dough.

4

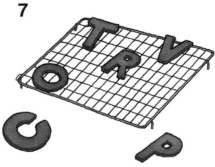

Sprinkle some flour on a work surface and place the dough on it. Roll it out until it is about 1cm (½in) thick.

5

Use a blunt knife.

Cut out the letters of your name. If you run out of dough, squeeze the scraps together and roll it again.

6

Slip a spatula under each letter and put it on the greased tray. Bake the letters for about 15 minutes.

7

Ask for help to take the letters out of the oven. Place them on a rack until they are cool.

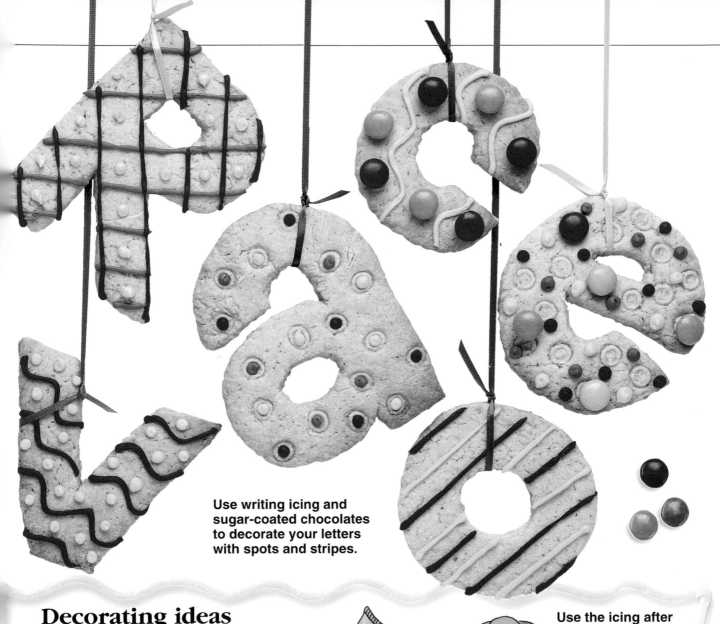

Use writing icing and sugar-coated chocolates to decorate your letters with spots and stripes.

Decorating ideas

Use the icing after your letters are cooked.

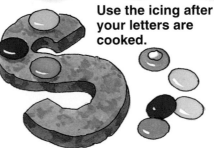

To make a spotted letter, press a clean pen top into the dough before you bake your letters.

When your letters have cooled, add lines and spots using writing icing. You can buy this in a supermarket.

Put a spot of icing on the back of a sugar-coated chocolate and then press it on your cooked letter.

Printing letters

Printing is a very quick way of making the same letter again and again.

Use a food tray with a pattern on it.

On these pages you will need:
A clean food tray
Pencil
Large paper or plain gift wrap
Kitchen sponge cleaning cloth
A clean plate
Paint or ink
Tape and scissors
Kitchen paper towel

1

Draw with a sharp pencil.

Carefully cut the bottom off the tray, then draw a letter the smooth side of it.

2

Tape the handle on the smooth side.

Lay your letter the correct way around.

Cut out your letter. Tape a strip of the tray onto your letter to make a handle.

3

Lay the sponge cloth on the plate and pour some runny paint or ink onto it.

4

Hold it by the handle.

Push your letter onto the paint on the cloth then press it onto your paper.

The striped letter was printed with bumpy cardboard instead of a food tray.

Use bright gift wrap instead of white paper.

Printed gift wrap

1

Cut a piece of gift wrap big enough to cover the parcel you are going to cover.

2

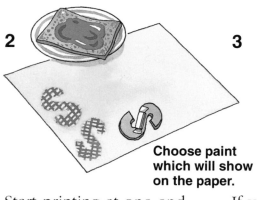

Choose paint which will show on the paper.

Start printing at one end. Press your letter in the paint each time you do a print.

3

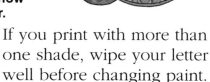

If you print with more than one shade, wipe your letter well before changing paint.

Printing in rows

1

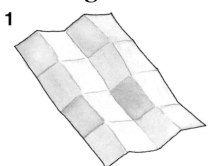

Fold a piece of paper to make sections following steps 1 and 2 on page 21.

2

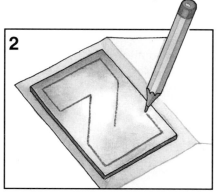

Cut some food tray slightly smaller than one of the sections. Draw a letter on it.

3

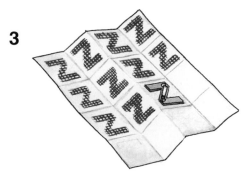

Cut out your letter and print one in each section of the folded paper.

Print an extra letter and glue it onto cardboard to make a gift tag.

Letters on a computer

You can use an art program on a computer to draw your own letters. Most art programs work in a similar way. Here you can find out how to draw letters with the Microsoft® Paintbrush™ program which you use with Microsoft® Windows®.

The Toolbox

You will find the Toolbox running down the left-hand side of your screen. Here are some of the things in the Toolbox which you can use to draw letters.

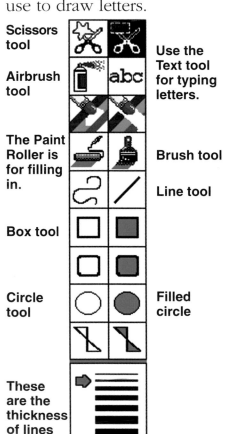

Scissors tool

Airbrush tool

Use the Text tool for typing letters.

The Paint Roller is for filling in.

Brush tool

Line tool

Box tool

Circle tool

Filled circle

These are the thickness of lines you can use.

1

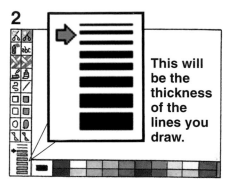

Pick this tool.

Mouse

Move the mouse so that an arrow points to the Brush tool. Click the left-hand button on the mouse.

2

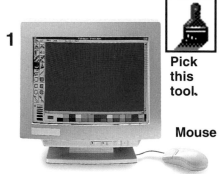

This will be the thickness of the lines you draw.

Choose one of the lines, then click the left-hand button on the mouse. The blue arrow will point to your line.

3

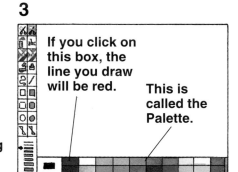

If you click on this box, the line you draw will be red.

This is called the Palette.

Move the arrow to the boxes along the bottom of the screen. Choose one of the boxes and click on it.

4

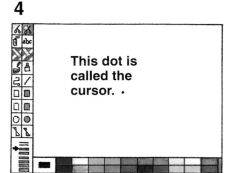

This dot is called the cursor. ·

Move the mouse so that a dot appears on your screen. Move the dot to the left-hand side of the screen.

5

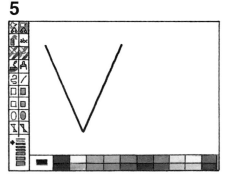

Put your finger on the left-hand button and hold it down. Draw a letter by moving the mouse.

6

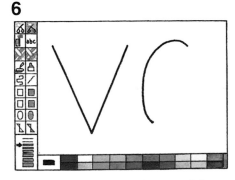

To draw another letter, lift your finger off the button, move the mouse and start again in a different place.

Filling in

Draw an outline of a letter on the screen. Make sure the ends of the lines are joined. Draw in any middle parts.

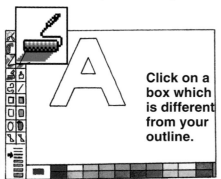

Click on a box which is different from your outline.

Click on the Paint Roller in the Toolbox. Then go down to the Palette at the bottom and click on a new box.

Move the mouse so that the tip of the roller is inside the outline of your letter. Click and your letter will fill in.

Letter ideas

You can draw all kinds of different letters on your computer. The different boxes in the Toolbox give you different shapes and effects. Here are a few for you to try.

Fill a red outline with red. Click on a new box in the Palette then click on the Circle tool. Hold your finger down and drag the mouse, then lift your finger.

Add lines with the Brush.

To add squares, pick the thickest line. Move the cursor to your letter and click on and off in different places.

Make a striped letter, using some thin and some thick lines.

To get a speckled letter, use the Airbrush tool.

Can you draw an E like this?

Design an alphabet

When you want to design something, you draw it and change it until you are happy with the way it looks. Why not try to design your own picture alphabet?

1

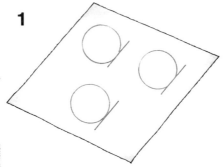

On scrap paper, draw some big letters faintly in pencil. Do the same letter two or three times.

2

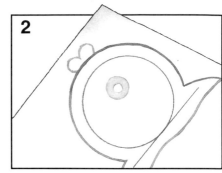

As you draw, think of which shapes you can use to make a round part or a tall straight part of a letter.

Alphabet ideas

Before you begin to design a picture alphabet, it's a good idea to choose a topic for your letters, such as animals or sports. Here are a few letters to give you some ideas.

A snake can bend to make different letters.

You could try to design a whole alphabet of snakes.

A name plate

Once you have designed your alphabet, you could use your new letters to make a name plate for a book or a door.

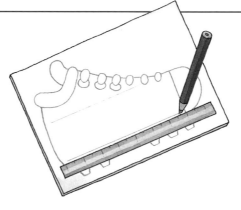

On the cardboard, draw an outline of a big shape. Draw two lines across it using a pencil and a ruler.

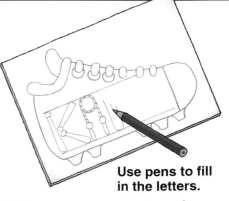

Use pens to fill in the letters.

Write your name using the letters you have designed. Use the lines as a guide for the size of your letters.

3

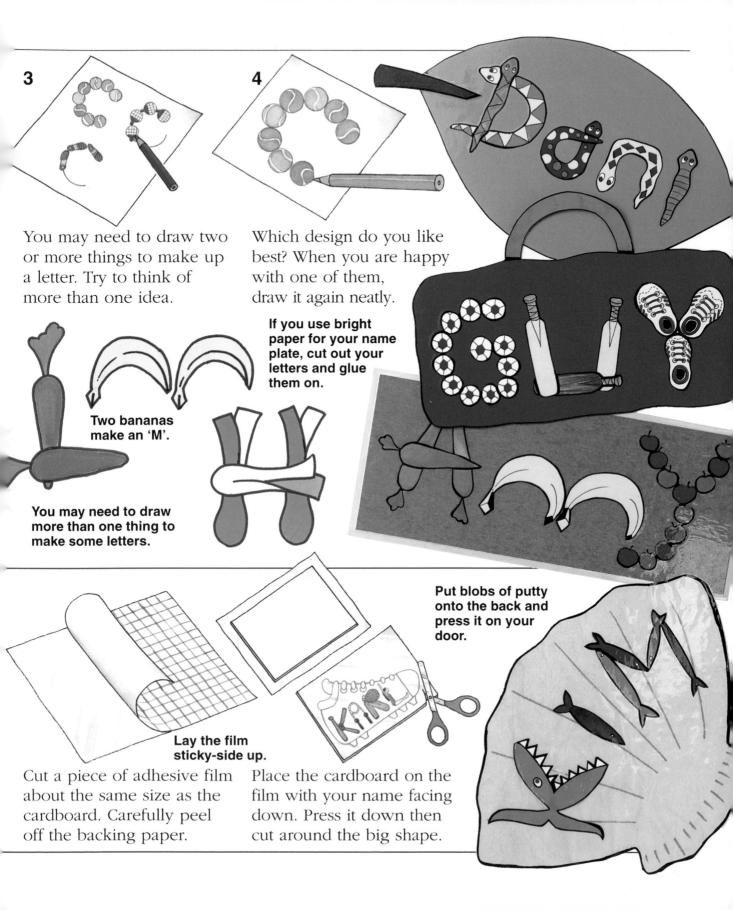

You may need to draw two or more things to make up a letter. Try to think of more than one idea.

Two bananas make an 'M'.

You may need to draw more than one thing to make some letters.

4

Which design do you like best? When you are happy with one of them, draw it again neatly.

If you use bright paper for your name plate, cut out your letters and glue them on.

Put blobs of putty onto the back and press it on your door.

Lay the film sticky-side up.

Cut a piece of adhesive film about the same size as the cardboard. Carefully peel off the backing paper.

Place the cardboard on the film with your name facing down. Press it down then cut around the big shape.

Looking at letters

Look around you. You can probably see lots of things with letters on them. You'll find all kinds of different lettering on books, comics and magazines, as well as on packets, clothes, posters and television. Look carefully at the letters. Each style has been chosen to suit the thing it is on.

OUT

STOP

Bus station

Bold letters are used to give information.

Some lettering looks as if it is making a noise.

CRASH

BOOM

Fireworks

On the beach

Castles

These letters give you an idea of what you might be reading about.

Lettering which catches your eye is used on posters and notices.

Letters in books

The different styles of letters which you see printed in books or magazines are called typefaces. Each typeface was designed by someone and has a name. The typeface you are reading now is called Garamond.
This typeface is called Kids.
This one is called Helvetica.
This one is called Bauhaus.

F — Serif

D

N S

These are sans serif letters.

Some typefaces have little lines at the ends of the letters. These lines are called serifs.

Letters which have no little lines are known as 'sans serif'. Can you see any other sans serif letters on this page?

Old lettering styles

If you visit a museum, try to find out if they have any old books or pictures with lettering on them. They may have some old books which have letters decorated with bright paint and real gold.

Letters like this one are called 'illuminated letters'.

Illuminated letters were often used to show where a new chapter started.

All the lettering was drawn and decorated by hand.

An illuminated letter

You could use bright felt-tip pens and a gold pen to draw an illuminated letter. Try to make the style of your letter look old.

You will need:
A pencil and a ruler
White or cream paper
Bright pens
A gold pen

Draw a large box with a pencil and a ruler. Add a letter to fill the box.

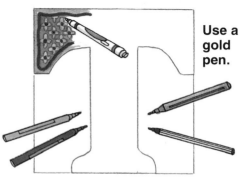

Use a gold pen.

Fill in the letter with tiny patterns. Add some patterns around the letter too.

A lettering book

You could keep a book with different types of lettering in it. Draw your own letters in the book or glue in ones you have written on pieces of paper.

You could also add lettering from old magazines, cards and packets.

Index

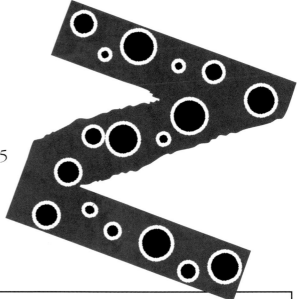

Acknowledgements

Pages 26 and 27: Screen shots reprinted with permission from Microsoft Corporation. Microsoft and Windows are registered trademarks of Microsoft Corporation. Paintbrush™ is a trademark of Wordstar Atlanta Technology Center.

Page 31: The illuminated letter at the top of the page, by courtesy of the Board of Trustees of the Victoria and Albert Museum. With thanks to Rita MacAdam, Elaine Brenchley and Christine Dyer.

First published in 1996 by Usborne Publishing Ltd, Usborne House, 83-85 Saffron Hill, London EC1N 8RT, England. Copyright © 1996 Usborne Publishing Ltd.

The name Usborne and the device 🎈 are Trade Marks of Usborne Publishing Ltd. All rights reserved.